Dear Parent:
Your child's love of reading starts here!

Every child learns to read in a different way and at his or her own speed. Some go back and forth between reading levels and read favorite books again and again. Others read through each level in order. You can help your young reader improve and become more confident by encouraging his or her own interests and abilities. From books your child reads with you to the first books he or she reads alone, there are I Can Read Books for every stage of reading:

SHARED READING
Basic language, word repetition, and whimsical illustrations, ideal for sharing with your emergent reader

BEGINNING READING
Short sentences, familiar words, and simple concepts for children eager to read on their own

READING WITH HELP
Engaging stories, longer sentences, and language play for developing readers

READING ALONE
Complex plots, challenging vocabulary, and high-interest topics for the independent reader

ADVANCED READING
Short paragraphs, chapters, and exciting themes for the perfect bridge to chapter books

I Can Read Books have introduced children to the joy of reading since 1957. Featuring award-winning authors and illustrators and a fabulous cast of beloved characters, I Can Read Books set the standard for beginning readers.

A lifetime of discovery begins with the magical words **"I Can Read!"**

Visit www.icanread.com for information
on enriching your child's reading experience.

I Can Read Book® is a trademark of HarperCollins Publishers.

Paddington: Meet Paddington

Based on the Paddington novels written and created by Michael Bond
PADDINGTON™ and PADDINGTON BEAR™ © Paddington and Company Limited/
STUDIOCANAL S.A. 2014
www.icanread.com

ISBN 978-0-06-234999-6

18 19 20 LSCC 10 9 8 7 6

First Edition

PADDINGTON™

Meet Paddington

Adapted by Annie Auerbach

Based on the screenplay written by Paul King

Based on the Paddington Bear novels

written and created by Michael Bond

HARPER

An Imprint of HarperCollinsPublishers

Hello. My name is Paddington.

I was born in Peru.

I came to London to find
a new home.

I stowed away on a ship.

After many days, I arrived

at Paddington Station.

At Paddington Station,

I met the Browns.

They took me home

to stay with them.

Mr. Brown is a serious man.

He protects his family

and likes things to be just so.

But he is also kind,
and he is willing to do
whatever it takes
to make people happy.

Mrs. Brown is an artist.
She noticed me in the station
and gave me my name.

She is helping me search

for a man who knew

my family.

Judy is the Browns' daughter.

She is sensitive

and keeps to herself.

It's hard to get to know new people,

but I hope she will be my friend.

Jonathan is Judy's
younger brother.
He is really interesting
and full of energy.

This family is very special.

They might be able

to give me a good home.

Mrs. Bird lives with the Browns.

She looks after them all.

She also knows a lot
about bears.

She makes sure I have
marmalade every day.

Mrs. Brown introduced me
to Mr. Gruber.
He owns an antiques shop
on Portobello Road.

Mr. Gruber is going
to help me find the man
who visited my aunt and uncle
in Peru.

I'm grateful to know
such nice people.
They are teaching me
many things about London.

But sometimes I still
find myself in hot water.
The Browns try
to understand my curiosity.

One person who is as curious

as I am is Millicent.

She works at

the Natural History Museum.

She researches all kinds of animals.

Millicent's father knew

my aunt and uncle.

She is very interested in me.

Millicent works with
the Browns' neighbor Mr. Curry.
He is not very fond of bears.

With Mr. Curry's help,

Millicent found me.

She offered to give

me a home.

I didn't realize she meant

a home in the museum

with her other animals.

Mrs. Brown found
the letter I left the family
telling them I had gone
to find the explorer.

The whole family came

to the museum

to rescue me.

When I set out from Peru,
I had no idea what adventures
I would find in England.

Mrs. Brown says
everyone is different.
That means everyone
can fit in.

I will never be like other people.

But that is because

I am a very unusual kind of bear.

A bear called Paddington.